This SCRIBBLERS

book belongs to:

....

This edition published in Great Britain in MMXIX
by Scribblers, an imprint of
The Salariya Book Company Ltd
25 Marlborough Place,
Brighton BN1 1UB
www.salariya.com

SALARIYA
SCRIBO BOOK HOUSE SCRIBBLERS

Text © Przemysław Wechterowicz MMXIX
Illustrations © Marianna Oklejak
Original English translations © Antonia Lloyd-Jones
First published in Polish in MMXI by G+J Gruner + Jahr Polska
English edition © The Salariya Book Company Ltd MMXIX

HB ISBN-13: 978-1-912537-95-2

1 3 5 7 9 8 6 4 2

A CIP catalogue record for this book is
available from the British Library.

Printed and bound in China

Printed on paper from sustainable sources

Visit
www.salariya.com
for our online catalogue and
free fun stuff.

Boom! Boom! Boom!

Przemysław Wechterowicz
Marianna Oklejak

SCRIBBLERS

a SALARIYA imprint

Two gorillas
And their chum
Beat their chests...
BOOM! BOOM!! BOOM!!!

BOOM BOOM
BOOM
BOOM BOOM
BOOM
Two gorillas
And their chum!

Two gorillas
And their chum
Make so much noise
Everybody comes
BOOM! BOOM!! BOOM!!!
BOOM! BOOM!! BOOM!!!

Two gorillas
And their chum!

Two gorillas
And their chum
Fill the air with
A mighty hum

BOOM! BOOM!! BOOM!!!
BOOM! BOOM!! BOOM!!!
Two gorillas
And their chum!

Pin your ears back
Hear it thumping
Soon the sound
Will have you jumping

BOOM! BOOM!! BOOM!!!

BOOM! BOOM!! BOOM!!!

Two gorillas

And their chum!

Daytime, nighttime
Father, mother
Winter, summer
Sister, brother

BOOM! BOOM!! BOOM!!!
BOOM! BOOM!! BOOM!!!
Two gorillas
And their chum!

You don't like it?
YES – you do…
Soon the sound will
Grab you, too

BOOM! BOOM!! BOOM!!!
BOOM! BOOM!! BOOM!!!

Two gorillas
And their chum!

High and low
Low and high
Point your nose up
To the sky

BOOM! BOOM!! BOOM!!!
BOOM! BOOM!! BOOM!!!

Two gorillas
And their chum!

Backward, forward
To and fro
Wave your hands
Tap your toes

BOOM! BOOM!! BOOM!!!
BOOM! BOOM!! BOOM!!!

Two gorillas
And their chum!

Now the rhythm's
Got you going
The town is buzzing
The sunset's glowing

BOOM! BOOM!! BOOM!!!
BOOM! BOOM!! BOOM!!!

Two gorillas
And their chum!

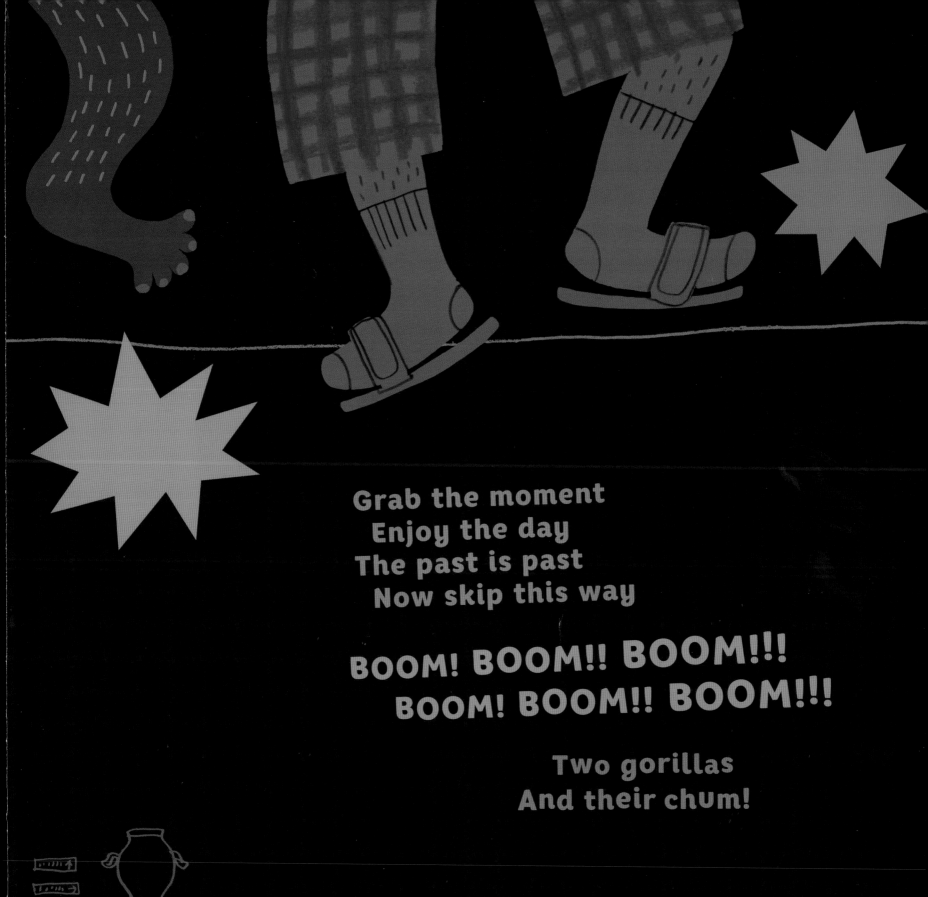

Grab the moment
Enjoy the day
The past is past
Now skip this way

BOOM! BOOM!! BOOM!!!
BOOM! BOOM!! BOOM!!!

Two gorillas
And their chum!

Wave your arms
Don't stop dancing
On the rooftops
Keep on prancing

BOOM! BOOM!! BOOM!!!
BOOM! BOOM!! BOOM!!!
Two gorillas
And their chum!

BOOM! BOOM!! BOOM!!!
BOOM! BOOM!! BOOM!!!
Two gorillas
And their chum!

Off to the Moon
To spread more fun

BOOM! BOOM!! BOOM!!!
BOOM! BOOM!! BOOM!!!

Two gorillas
And their chum!

Things to find

Can you find these things by looking closely at the pages?

A baboon

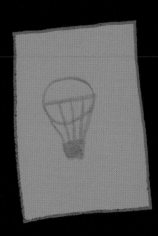

A hot air balloon

A crab

An antelope

An elephant

A helicopter

A bat

A flying
roast chicken

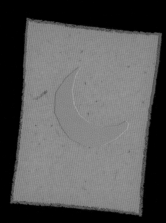

The Moon

A television